I Know But I Just Don't Know
A Story of Just Don't Think About It

Yahya Jongintaba author illustrator

Written and designed at
Jongintaba Ecovillage
Morogoro Tanzania
East Africa
May 2023

ISBN: 9798394961762

There is an infinite ever-youthful knowing within all of us but we do not know what it is or how it works and yet it attracts us. If this ever-youthful knowing did not attract us we would not go into it for who goes into something they do not know? Courageous persons go into things they do not know but even their courage is something unknown to them while yet it is known.

—I Know but I Just Don't Know

Speech of the Old Man to His Grandson

Why do I sometimes answer you with "Just don't think about it?" Because "because" just keeps on going on and on and on
    because there are things you can know and yet not be sure about and thinking about them simply does not help. There must be another approach to certainty other than thinking when thinking is just more labor in a direction that opposes sure knowing. There must be another approach to certainty and there must be another certainty other than that which thinking thinks it comes up with
    because the certainty that thinking conceives is surely showing itself to be labor-intensive and still inconclusive. Which is better when what is certain is that thinking makes for so much tediousness and tiredness and on the other hand so much terrorizing toughness?
    because not-thinking is surely not to be blamed for terrifying toughness when obviously it is thinking that causes terrible things to happen. You can see quite clearly that terrible-things-doers always leave a thinking-trail

because thinking is always done on the surface. It is not deep it is not hidden it is not closed but quite open and quite public and therefore quite accessible because it is conditioned by and therefore always aimed at fitting into and speaking to the general audience that is its market. The general audience dogs and dogs for more thinking more thinking-productivity more doing and doing of endless cognitive processing

because thinking is entertaining. There is nothing else to do but to be entertained when just sitting in the general audience all the general time. Some of thinking is creative some of it pedantic and paralyzingly boring but even boring thinking is entertaining when it keeps the mind busy enough to prevent it from sliding into repose. No one wants their mind to slide into repose

because it is not widely known what the repose is where the repose goes and what the repose's consequences are because no pedantic person has yet come up with anything definite that the general audience wants to think about without having to think too much. Maybe the consequence of repose could be called "thought" in contrast to "thinking" where thinking is furiously laborious and thought comes freely effortless and unexpectedly as a message from somewhere out there or somewhere in here but who cares

    because thought comes without ferocious labor? You do not have to care about it or think about it or labor over it and ruin it with thinking. This is the thing to realize with certainty which you need not think about because it is obvious. Thinking really has been ruinous. Should it not be admitted that most of what is free of ruin has come from thought. Just wait and see

    because you see I am not trying to force thinking on you like so many ferocious people. No one wants to think about all the forcing of thinking and actually no one should think about it but just wait and see it. Wait and see thinking for what it shows itself truly to be and let the seed of what is seen sow itself into the dark soil of the earthy mind where under the right conditions of sunshine it will grow

    which is so refined a process in the mind of the human of nature that it is best not to think about it but just to wait don't you think? Just don't think about it because

1

All kinds of people are going around saying "I know but I just don't know" and doing things they say cannot be explained. Previously unknowable and unfathomable was the phenomenon of human beings rising into the sky and flying and yet here was a man and woman doing this very thing. Not only were there no wings attached to this man and woman but they had not even a complete set of arms. Asking them what made them think they could fly without wings or even complete arms led them only to answer with another popular saying of the day "Just don't think about it." Pressed to explain at least a little of the I-know-but-I-just-don't-know" the flying people pointed down to a mountain forest and spoke of a rumored old man some 108 years of age who allegedly had said that "I know but I just don't know" could save the world and heal the weary soul.

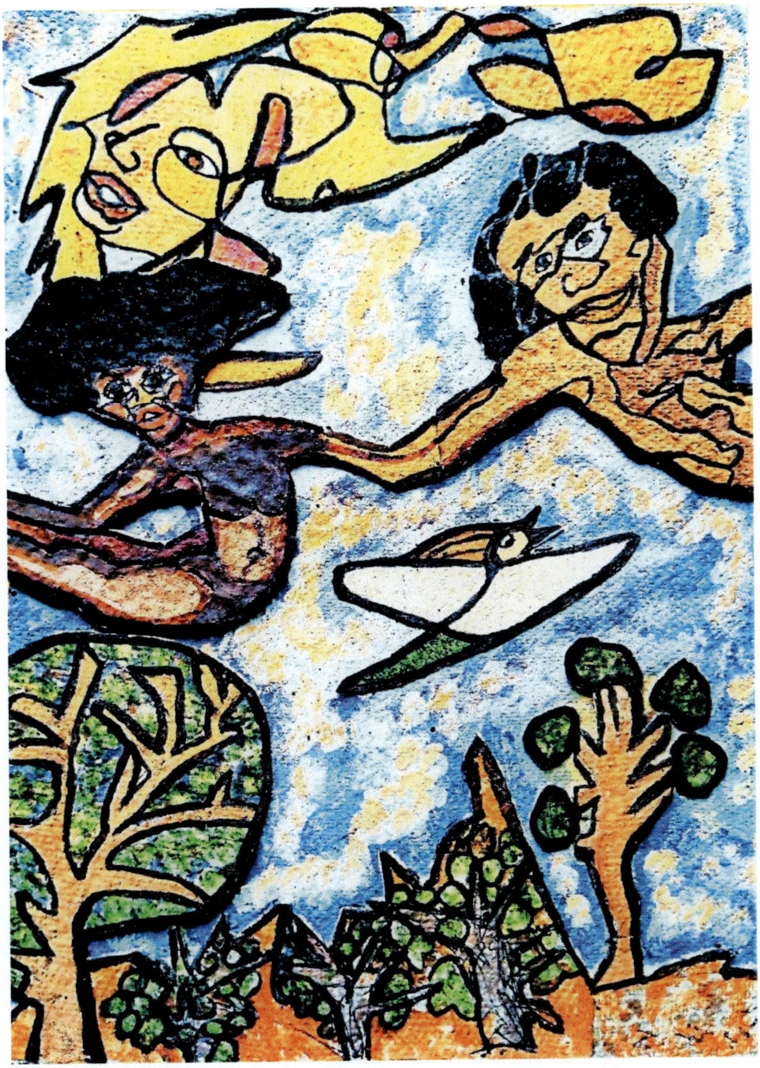

2

At the wonder of seeing nearly armless people taking to the skies and now flying one another as kites the sun had even to take note and ask the kiters what made them think they could fly and fly high and why. "I know but I just don't know" was the answer and when the sun asked the child flying close to him how he could know and not know at the same time the child pointed down to the mountain forest and said "Just don't think about it." When the sun pressed the child with the question of whether school had taught him to think this way his father cut in and spoke of the rumored old man some 108 years of age alleged to have started the I-know-but-I-just-don't-know craze. When the sun asked what more was known about the rumored old man the father said "Even if we knew a little about him the problem would come when we think about it."

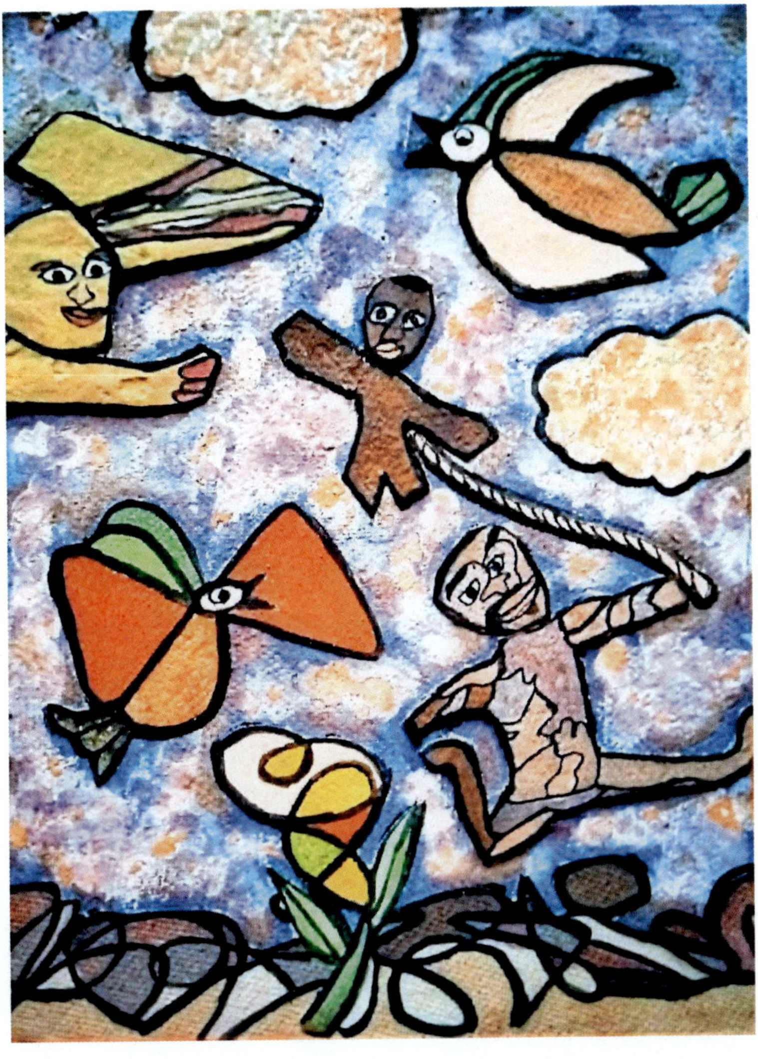

3

When asked about the old man alleged to have started the whole I-know-but-I-just-don't-know craze some flying people insisted it was best to go see the old man who lived in the mountain forest with his wife and child. As a consequence of increasing numbers of people going into the forest to find the old man there came out of the forest fantastic stories in which each storyteller seemed bent on outdoing all others. One forest veteran said the 108-year-aged man was a mystic who along with his family ate one vegetarian meal a day and drank only water for which reason he was exceedingly healthy strong and young-looking. As for the meaning of "I know but I just don't know" the forest veteran quoted the old man as saying "There is an infinite ever-youthful knowing within all of us but we do not know what it is or how it works and yet it attracts us. If this ever-youthful knowing did not attract us we would not go into it for who goes into something they do not know? Courageous persons go into things they do not know but even their courage is something unknown to them while yet it is known."

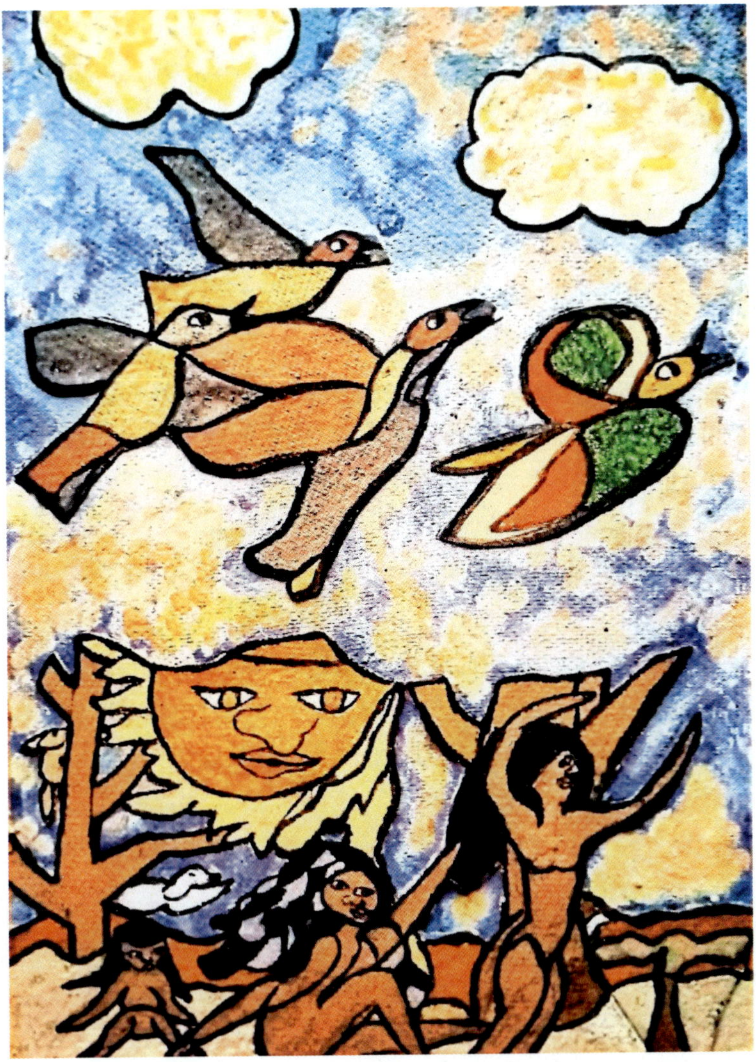

4

Another veteran of the mountain forest said the mystic was an old tree that turned him into a tree also so he could understand the tree talk regarding the wisdom he sought. Even before this story could be completed there were already listeners asking "How is this possible?" in contrast to others preferring "I know but I just don't know" followed by "Just don't think about it." The story did not get any less I-just-don't-knowish when this forest veteran detailed the tree talk he had with the mystic. "'Who are you?' the old tree asked me. Without thinking I answered 'I know but I just don't know.' The old tree asked 'What is your name?' I answered 'I know but I just don't know.' The old tree asked 'Where are you from?' I answered 'I know but I just don't know.' After this went on for a while the old tree said "Go to your mother and father and say to them 'I know but I just don't know.' I did as the mystic had directed said to my parents these words and my mother gleefully responded 'O my son how we know but we just don't know that we love you. Isn't it wonderful.' The family answered together 'It's wonderful.'"

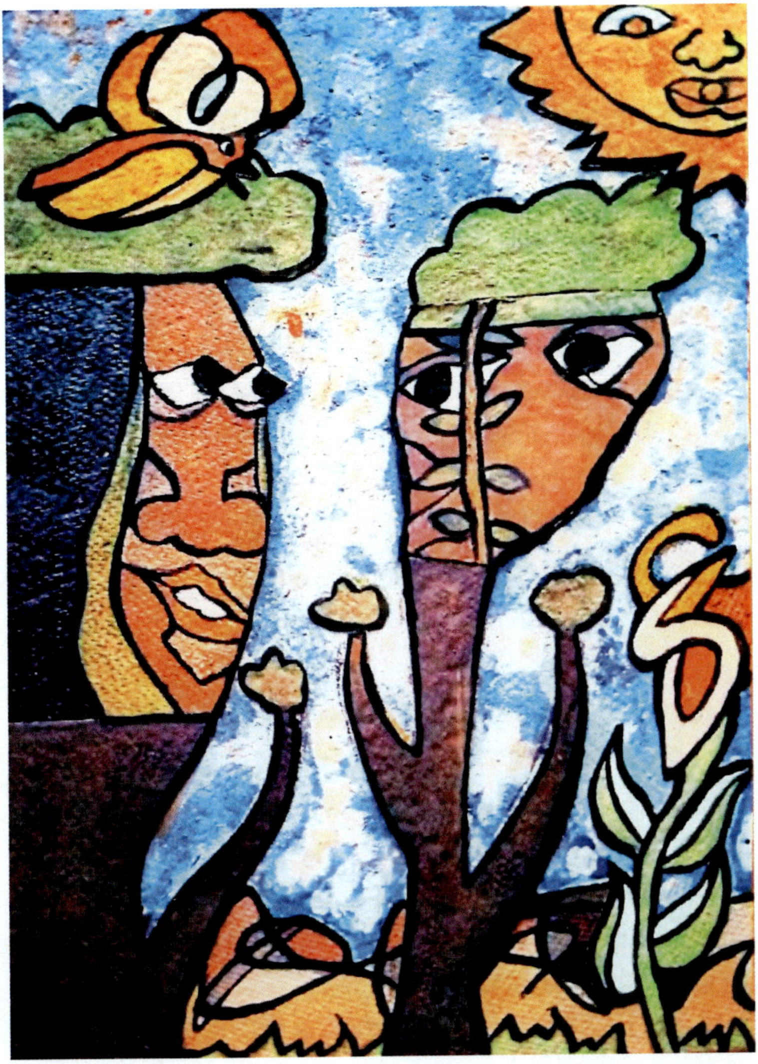

5

What the previous person reported of his encounter with the old mystic in the mountain forest might not have been "quite accurate" according to another mountain forest veteran who said he had found the old man to be not himself a tree but one who dispensed his wisdom perched upon a tree that appeared to be his rumored wife. "When I asked the mystic about his relationship to the tree he said 'So what might love be? Might it be the I-know-but-I-just-don't-know that attracts you in a way that you cannot know while yet you know because it is faith that does the knowing? and might it be that the feeling of faith is the feeling of love?'" The rest of this forest-veteran's story was basically the same as the previous veteran's story. He said "I was directed to go tell my mother and father 'I know but I just don't know.' I did as the mystic said and told my parents and they responded joyously 'O our son how we know but we just don't know that we love you. Isn't it wonderful' and for some reason I did feel wonderful and deeply at peace."

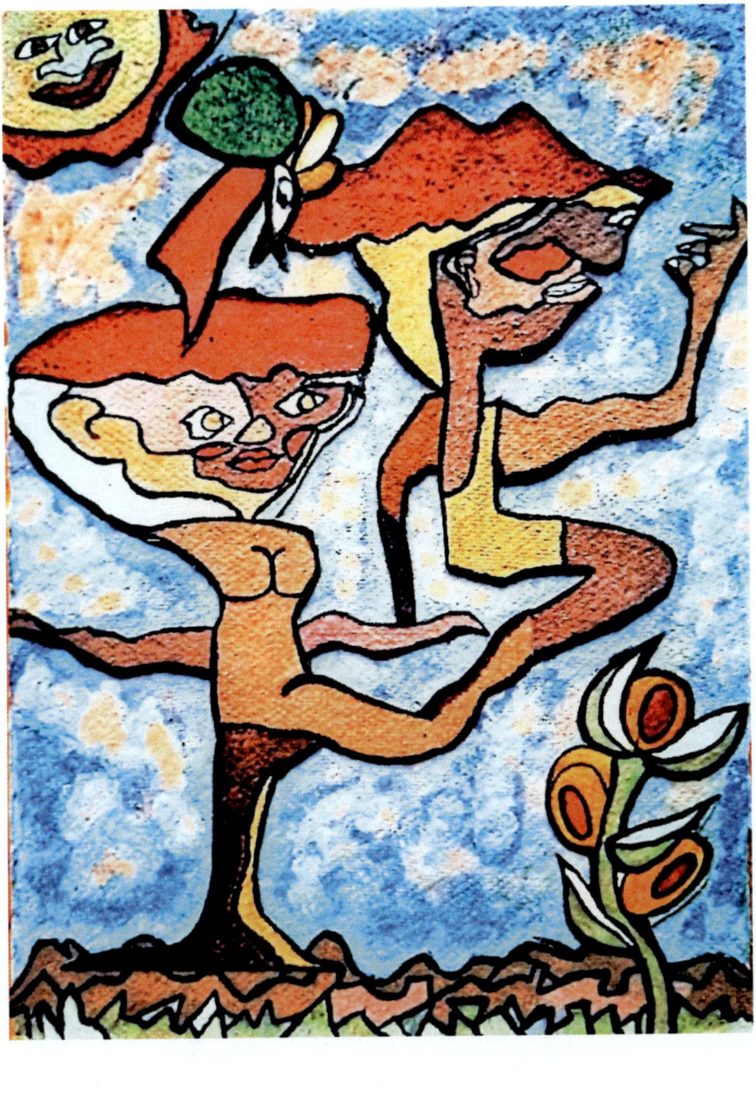

6
Previous stories of mountain forest veterans had been relatively sensible and reasonable compared to later stories for next-up returning from the forest was a group of youths who claimed the old mystic threw huge I-know-but-I just-don't-know sky-parties for which the mystic's wife played the guitar and everyone danced wildly like they did not know anything including how to dance. As proof of their mystical party-experience the youths broke out into the song they said the old-man mystic had started singing "to stir up the craze in the stuck-up world"

*I know but I just don't know
know but I just don't know
This is love isn't it?*

*I know but I just don't know
know but I just don't know
I feel like in heaven.*

*I know but I just don't know
know but I just don't know
Where in heaven you are?*

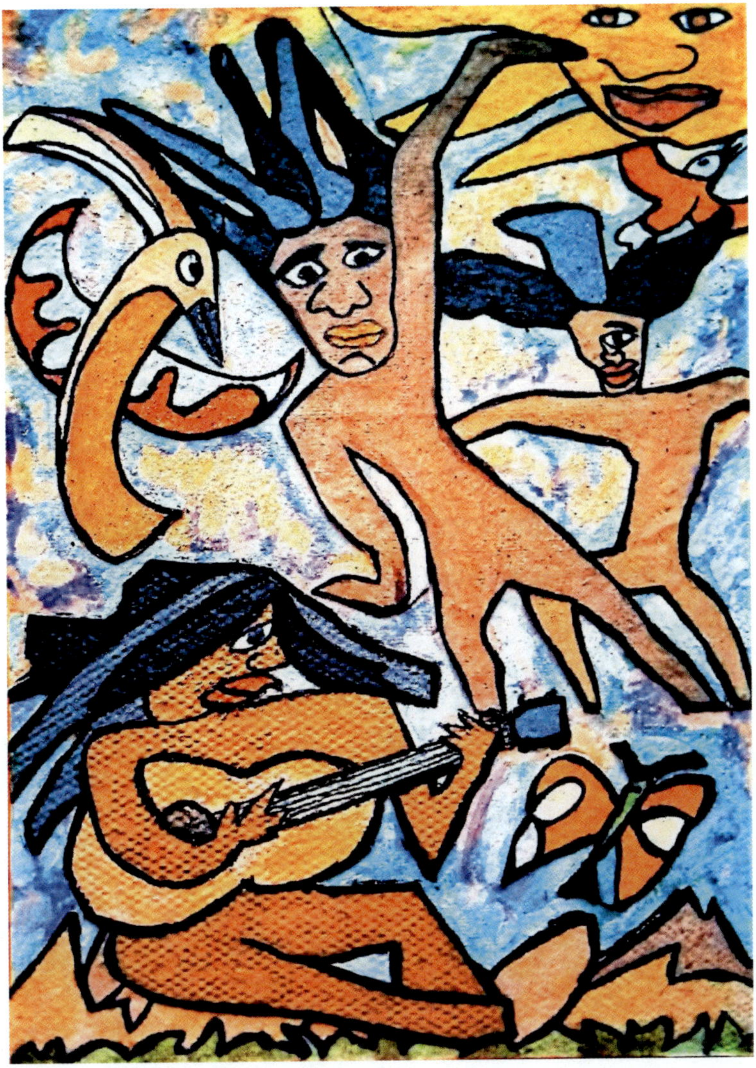

7

Other youths came forth with varying accounts of the mystic's I-know-but-I just-don't-know sky-partying. They reported that the mystic's wife did not just play the guitar but with her husband had gotten so intoxicated on I-know-but-I just-don't-know that together they sang and danced like maniacs who did not know anything. One thing that was common in the telling of all these stories of increasing fantasticness is that among story-listeners were people who wanted to know the truth but who in the meantime just shrugged in wonder and said "Just don't think about it." The story did not get any less I-just-don't-knowish when these storytelling youths went on to report of the mystic's party-wisdom about the singing and dancing from his mystical mouth and mystical limbs for the mystic had said "I wonder what these sounds and movements mean? Is not 'I know but I just don't know' a more honest and humble way of living by staying with the question rather than trying to force an answer? And what does that mean? Just don't think about it and throughout life just dance and sing faithfully."

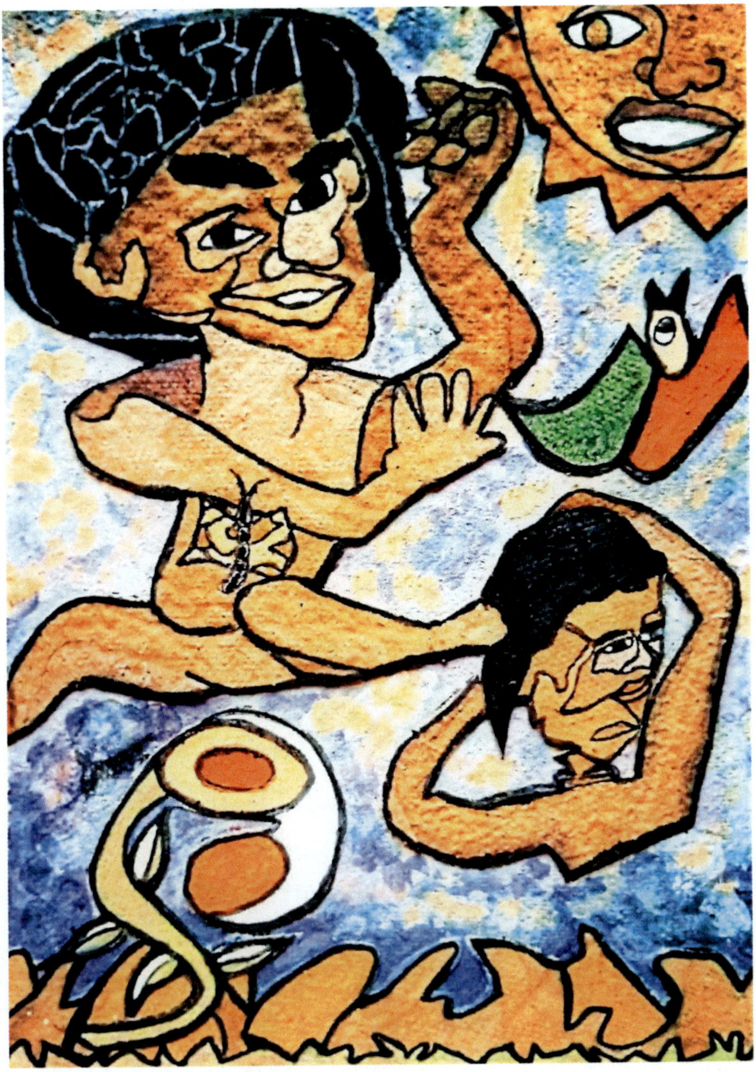

8
That increasingly fantastic stories portrayed the mystic and his wife as capable of the wildest singing and dancing at the I-know-but-I just-don't-know sky-parties seemed to counter the idea of the mystic being anywhere close to 108 years old. But the alleged contradiction was clapped back at by some elders in the audience who borrowed the phrase "Just don't think about it" and themselves quoted some of the mystic's words they had heard "There is an infinite ever-youthful knowing within all of us but we do not know what it is or how it works and yet it attracts us." The elder who did the quoting paused and then added "About this we could say that this infinite ever-youthful knowing of which the mystic spoke draws us into its own youthfulness because we are no longer stressed about knowing stuff so we can now accept life as simply a question to ask." The youths looked at one another in wonder and ask this elder "What are you talking about?" to which the elders shook their heads and answered all together "I know but I just don't know Just don't think about it."

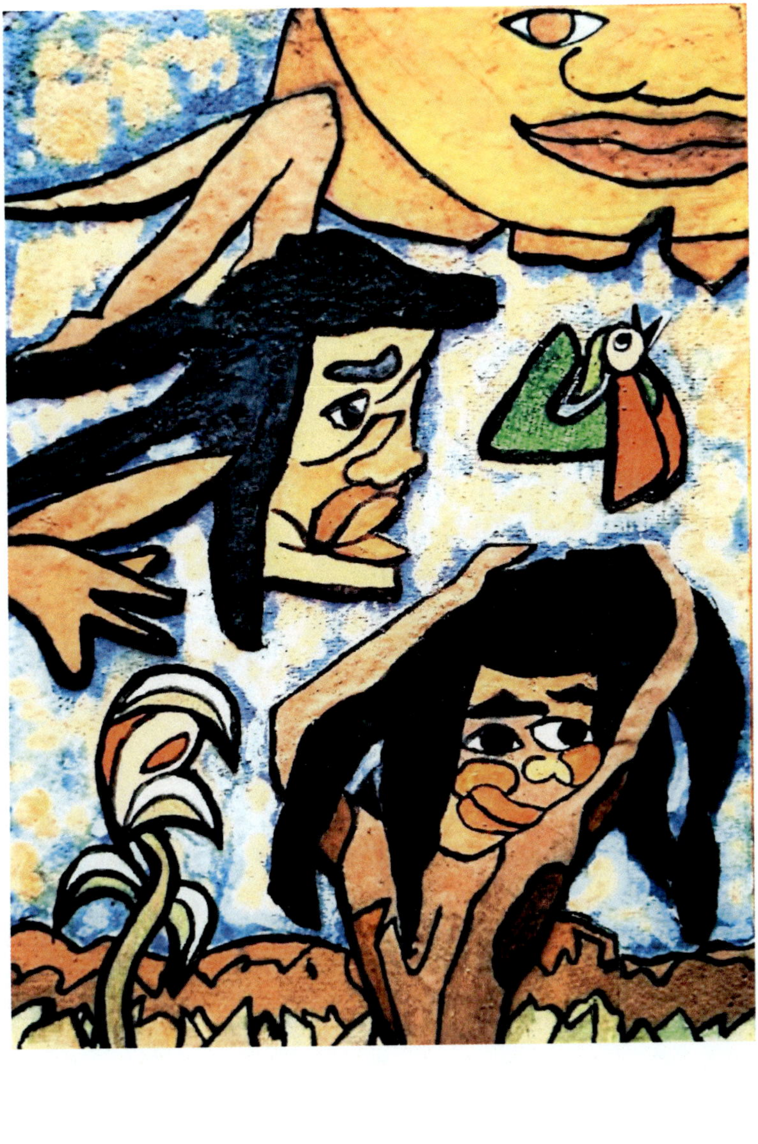

9

One group of youths who were part of a recent youth excursion into the mountain forest said that the mystic's I-know-but-I-just-don't-know parties were not in the sky but on the ground and that it was not only the mystic and his wife who sang and danced wildly but all of nature in the mountain-forest as if nature knew nothing about song and dance and how song and dance are to be done. Yet nature does know something of song and dance because the mystic had said "It is from nature that human beings learned song and dance and it is in the shadow of nature that human beings conclude regarding the origins of song and dance 'I know but I just don't know.' What can be said of nature's original song and dance except 'I know but I just don't know Just don't think about it'? So just listen to the music and dance."

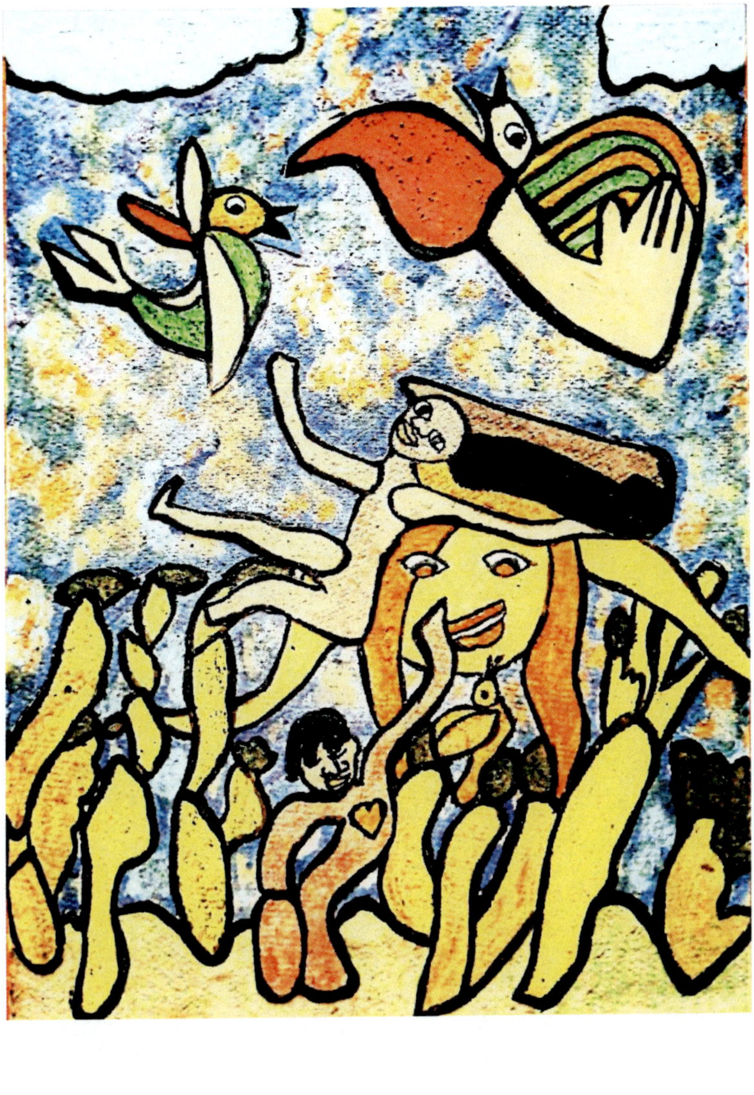

10

Other youths who had gone into the mountain forest searching out the mystic added to the former story saying that nature not only sang and danced with the mystic but also did the mystic's talking. They had only gotten fleeting glimpses of the mystic himself as he and his wife flitted about in the bush each under the illumination of their own sun so it was nature that spoke for the old man. In answer to their questionings about how and why nature did the mystic's talking nature itself answered in the mystic's behalf "Nature speaks because 'I know but I just don't know' is not common talk. It is not common talk but there is in nature's talk something that already meets the criteria of mystery and the necessity of people understanding it. You can listen to nature therefore and feel quite alright about knowing without knowing what nature is saying."

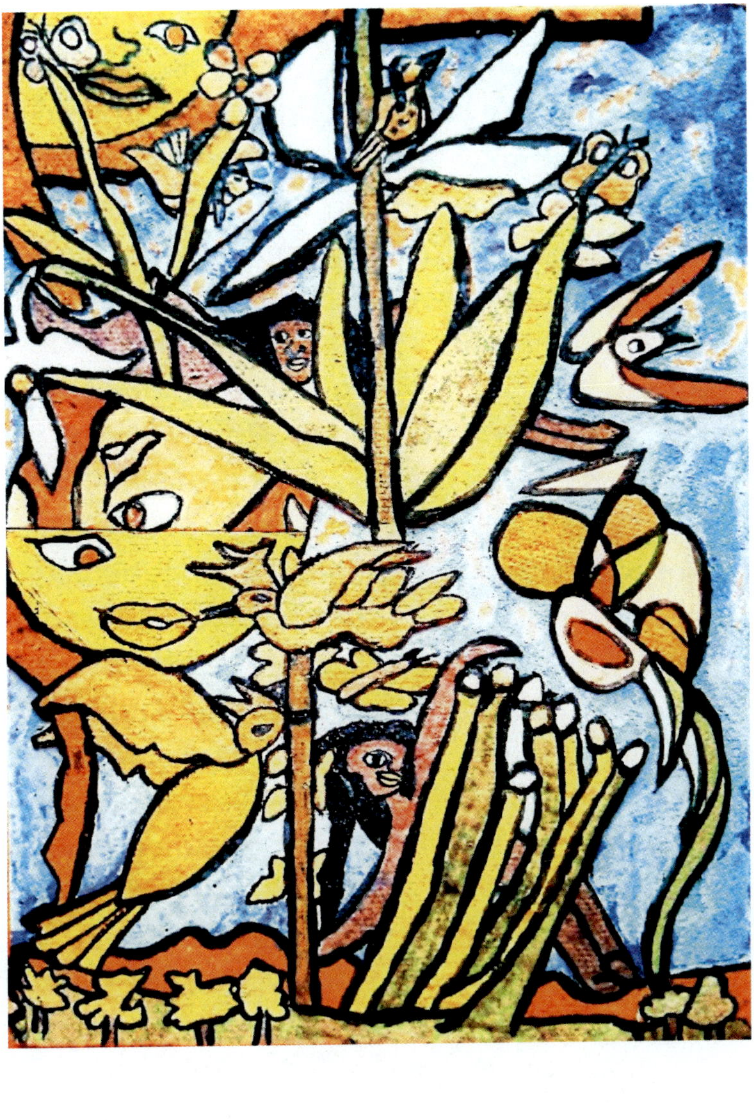

11

Given an earlier report that the old mountain-forest mystic and his wife were each illumined by their own sun various mountain forest veterans started coming out with even more fantastic stories. One story claimed that the mystic and his wife were "sun people" with skin burnt a supple light brownish-yellow and that the mystic did not speak through his mouth but through the illumination of his sunny dreadlocks. When the mystic was asked about this communicative phenomenon his sunlocks themselves answered luminously in his behalf "You feel the rays and warmth of all sunlit love because you are the sunlight of the world. You are the sunlight of the world that exudes warm love from all your pores. If you were not the sunlight of the world then whence comes the glory that you give? If you are alive then you are part of the Glorious All brilliantly sunshining and you too will grow sunlocks and warmly answer all questioners with the ultimate brilliance of 'I know but I just don't know Just don't think about it.'"

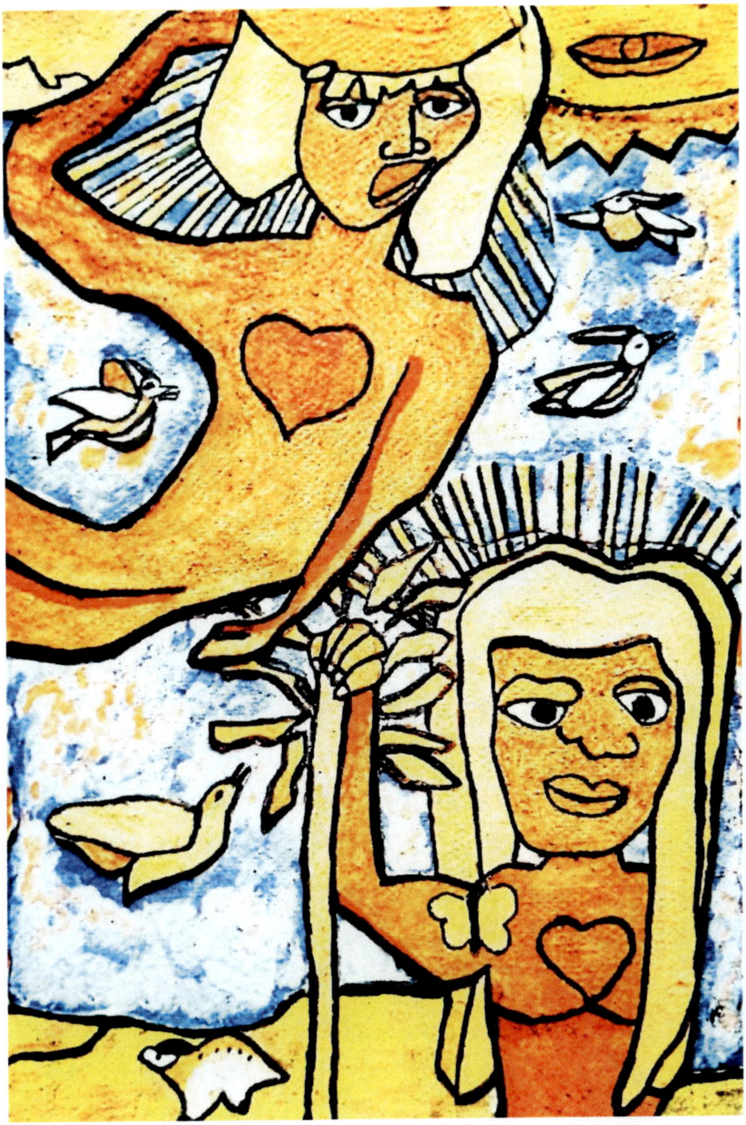

12

Other youths who went into the mountain forest said that the mystical sun-man had not a body but just a head and that he was not burnt a light brownish yellow but a dark yellowish-brown that made him unmistakably a "negro sun." This mystical negro sun-man did not speak directly to them they said but only to disciples he had transformed into trees capable of remaining in a single place long enough to receive his sunrays of wisdom. "As a tree you just don't know why my sunrays make you grow" the mystic said to one tree-disciple "and yet you know to receive the sunrays and gather their energy as each ray shines to you through the forest of trees. Why else would sunrays shine to you one at a time like one thought after another precipitates like rain? You know but you just don't know that the sunrays of wise thought shine to you so you can receive each of them and gather them together for more and more knowing because ultimate knowing is too big to handle all at one time. You know but you just don't know Just don't think about it."

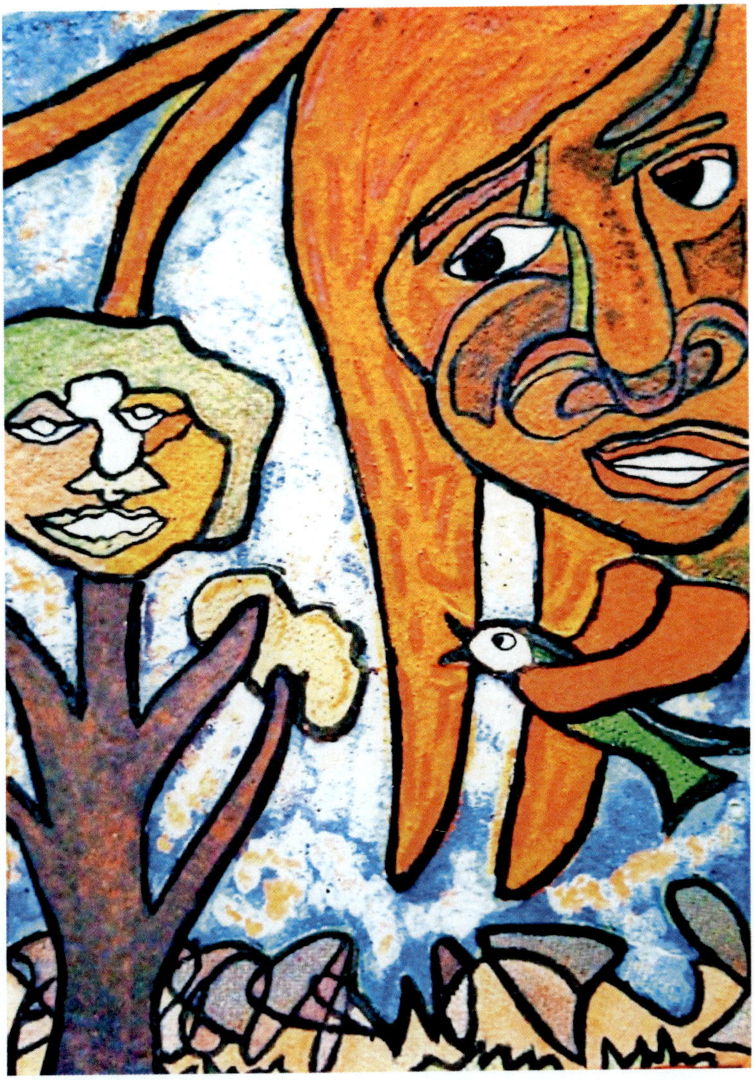

13

Some mountain forest veterans verified that the mystic was in fact a "negro sun" but added that the person always with him was his wife and that she was not herself a sun but just a regular colored woman a little abnormal. Her face reflected the color-spectrum of light-wisdom her husband's sun-gaze constantly set upon her and so it was she who spoke colorfully in the mystic's behalf when asked about her abnormality "Your own inner colorfulness is hidden from you and yet you know but you don't know that it is there. The hiddenness of what you know of your inner coloredness is fruitful for you because you can never be limited by what you know taking the dull colorless form of solidified knowledge. Always then you can live with soulful color beyond what you know without knowing it. Always then all things are spectacularly possible.'"

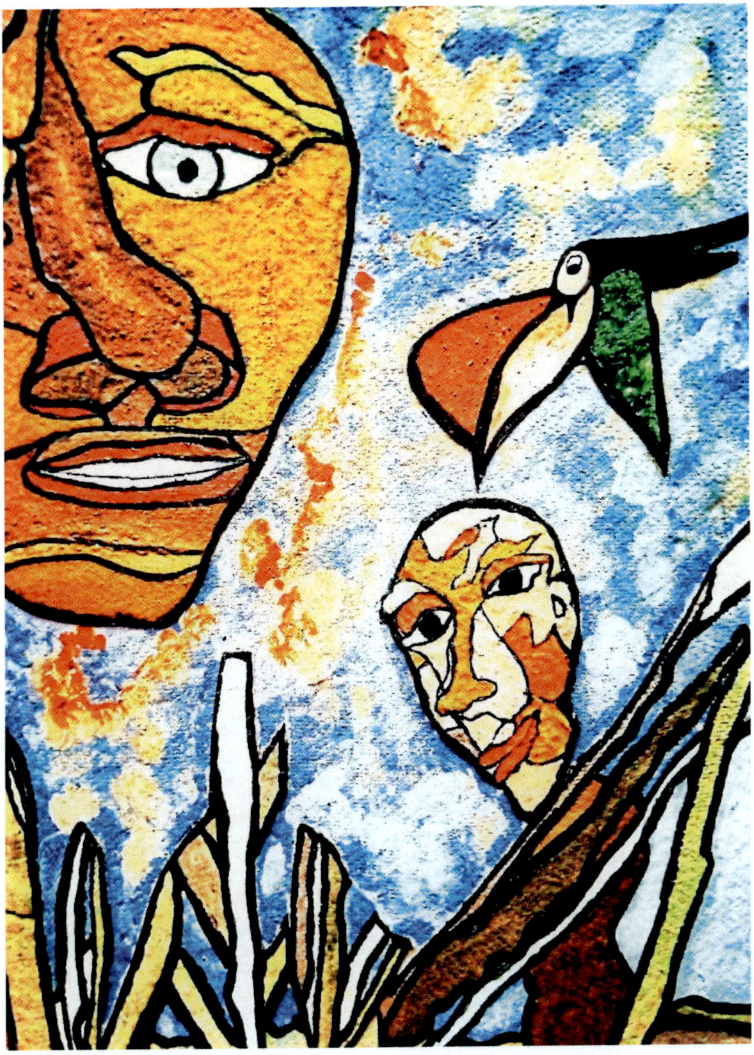

14

Disabled people who went into the mountain forest reported that at the time of sunset the large orb of the "negro sun" turned back into the full-bodied old man who with his stored sun-energy would lay a soulful hand on people needing healing. When the listeners of these stories inquired as to the means by which people were soulfully healed the storytellers quoted the mystic as having raised his soul-hand and having through that hand spoken of the healing power of "I know but I just don't know." The mystic's raised hand had said "'I know but I just don't know' takes no effort and takes no time but ceases time wherever it enters. In this timeless stand-stillness my soul-hand exists in calm attentiveness such calm attentiveness that healing attends without any healed one knowing it has happened. 'I know but I just don't know' is all that healed ones can say and it is itself a handy healing word."

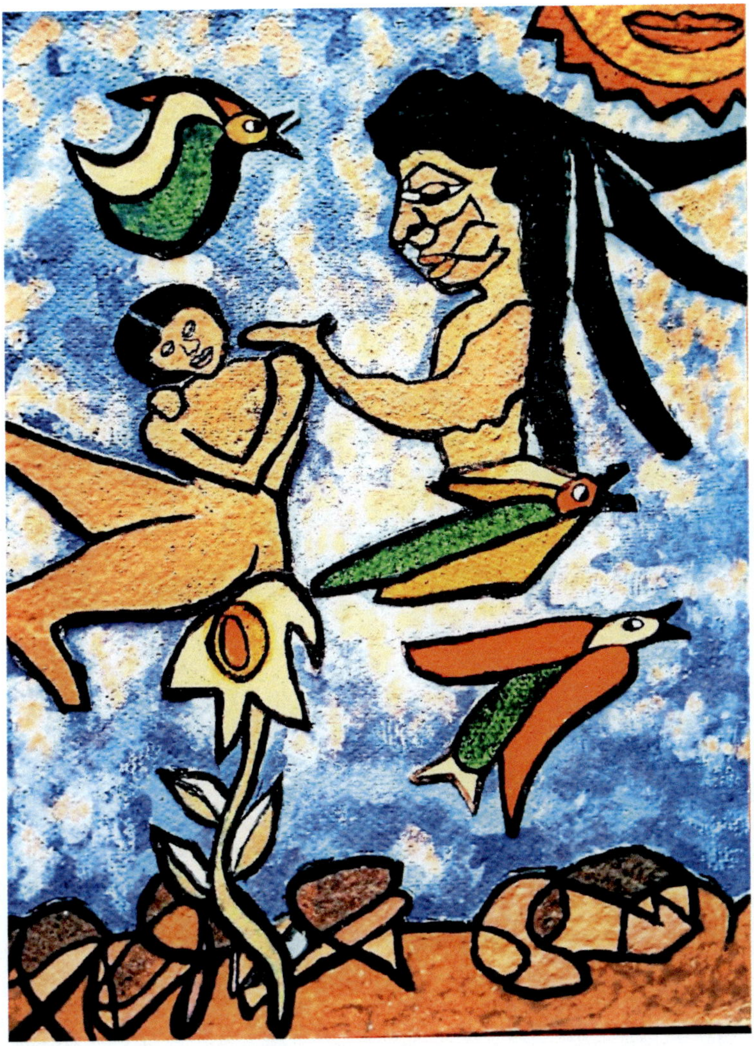

15

One thing in common about all of the fantastic story-tellings about the alleged old-man mountain-forest mystic is that among story-audiences were always people who wanted to know the truth and hardly a soul who knew the truth or told the truth until a particular day a youth came from a storytelling audience holding the hand another youth who had shouted "What is the truth to all this craziness?" The two youths walked away from the ruckus caused by the question and the one who knew the truth said "I know the truth because the so-called sun man mountain-forest man mystic man is my grandfather and the woman rumored to be with him is his daughter my mother." "Is your granddad the mystic?" "I once asked him and he said he did not know what a mystic was because a mystic was so mysterious that he could only say 'I know but I just don't know.'" "So your grandfather started the craziness?" "The crazy story actually began with my mother when she asked her father my grandfather a challenging question and he ventured an answer."

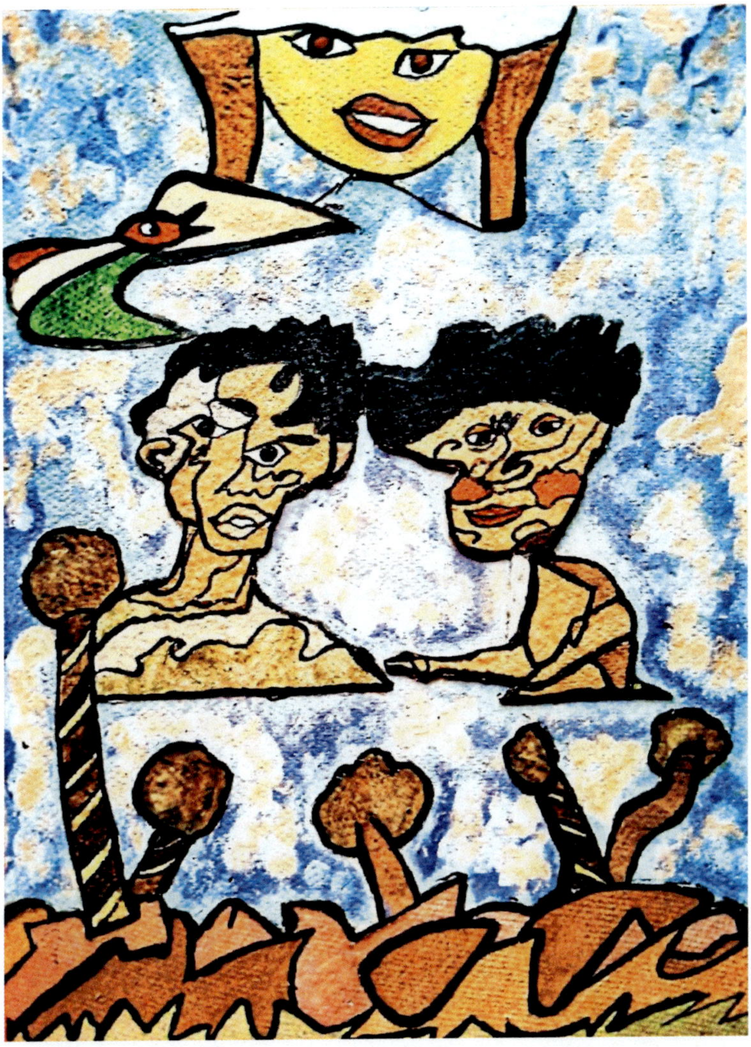

16

"My father I have countless questions to ask you about life but how can I possibly ask all of them and how can you possibly answer? Will you remain with me forever?" Thoughtfully the father answered his beloved daughter "Perhaps there is one great answer that can be given to you for all your questions if the questions are substantive but the answer only raises more questions that will nag at you. Do you want to know that one answer to all substantive questions and all so-called answers?" The daughter said "I want to know this one answer so please tell me what is it?" The father said "Then I will tell you a little story."

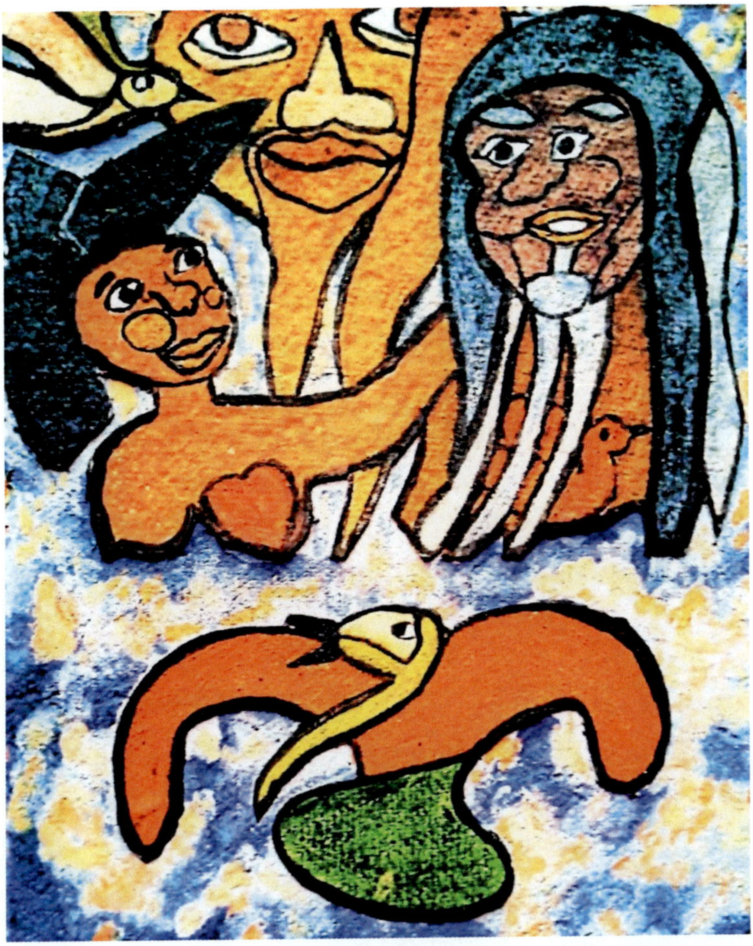

17

"Ninety years ago when I first saw your mother and we were both eighteen years of age I was playing my drum and she listened long to my drum talk. My drumming spoke to her heart so she came up close touched my head and said 'I think you love me.' I said to the beat of my drum 'I know but I just don't know.' She said 'What do you mean by that?' I said with my drum 'Let's sing to see if we can understand it' and we sang *'I know but I just don't know. I know but I just don't know. I know but I just don't know.'* She sang and said 'This is love isn't it?' and we continued to sing *'I know but I just don't know. I know but I just don't know.'* She said 'I feel like I am in heaven.' *'I know but I just don't know. I know but I just don't know.'* I answered 'Do you know where in heaven you are?' *'I know but I just don't know. I know but I just don't know'.* She said 'I am lost in the heavenly song.' *'I know but I just don't know. I know but I just don't know'.* I said 'Yes this is what love is.'"

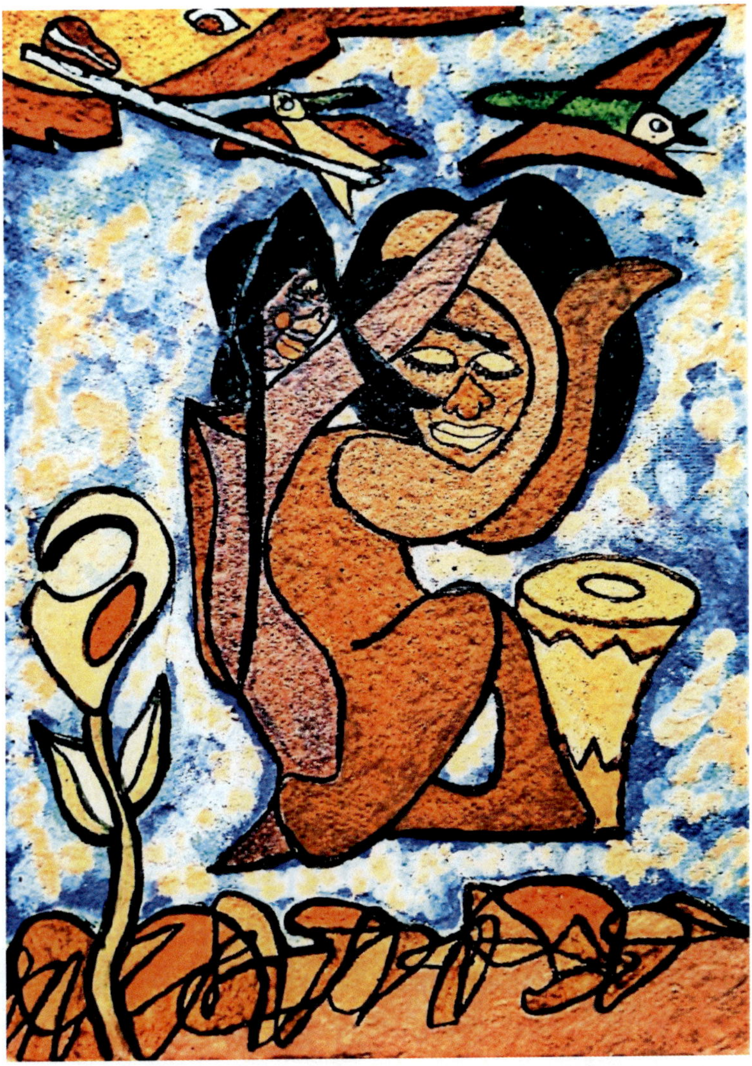

18

"My father how did this mysterious one great answer come to you for the answering of all substantive questions?" The father answered "It came to me one day in a dream in which I was playing my guitar maybe around forty-five years of age. I was dreaming of playing my guitar and dreaming of the woman I would one day love. In that dream with my guitar-playing I asked myself 'How do I know this is the right woman I see?' and the answer came to me 'I know but I just don't know.'" The daughter said "O how I love this story my father but I have one more question hoping there is one more answer you can give to address the one great answer 'I know but I just don't know.' Father what really is meant by this?" The father said "I thought you would ask so I saved for last the greater answer that is even an answer to the great answer 'I know but I just don't know.'" The daughter said "I want to know this greater answer so please tell me what is it?" He said "Just don't think about it" and together they sang

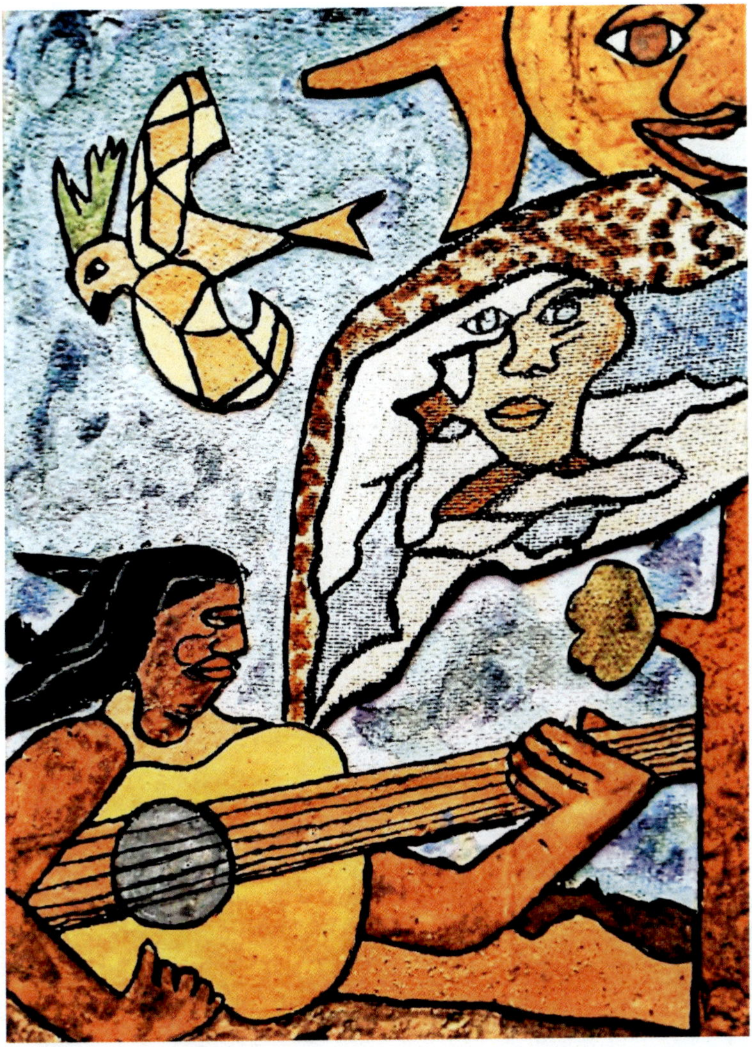

*I know but I just don't know
know but I just don't know
This is love isn't it?*

*I know but I just don't know
know but I just don't know
I feel like I am in heaven.*

*I know but I just don't know
know but I just don't know
Do you know where you are?*

Conclusion

Just don't think about it.

Made in the USA
Middletown, DE
28 May 2023